Lucy The Cat Christmas

PERTTI A PIETARINEN

ISBN-13: 978-1517153700
ISBN-10: 1517153700

DEDICATION

This Book is dedicated to Aleksi, Ellen, Marcus and Katariina

And of course to

Lucy The Cat

Read other books from Pertti A Pietarinen:

Lucy The Cat: ISBN 978-1494444136, 2014
http://www.amazon.com/dp/B00IARLDCY
God's Children: ISBN 978-1497567399, 2014
http://www.amazon.com/dp/B00JPT3L4O
Lucy The Cat: Little Brother: ISBN 978-1500770396, 2014
http://www.amazon.com/dp/B00MQI99N8
Lucy The Cat Play With Me: ISBN 978-1505607000, 2015
http://www.amazon.com/dp/B00STTT01Y
Lucy The Cat And Little Kittens: ISBN 978-1515385288, 2015
http://www.amazon.com/dp/B014FPTOM0
Lucy The Cat Christmas: ISBN 978-1517153700, November 2015

Books in Finnish and in Japanese:
Kissa Kiiskinen sankarina ja muita satuja: ISBN 978-9522303141, Aurinko Kustannus Oy, 2014
Lucy-kissa, Lucy The Cat: ISBN 978-1497535633, 2014
http://www.amazon.com/dp/B00JPSSY2E
Lucy-kissa ja pikkuveli: ISBN 978-1502764096, 2014
http://www.amazon.com/dp/B00OHDBYW4
Lucy-kissa leiki kanssani: ISBN 978-1507563403, 2015
http://www.amazon.com/dp/B00STZ3CRQ
Lucy-Kissa ja pikku sisarukset: ISBN 978-9523189782, 2015
http://www.amazon.com/dp/B015SRKNDS
Lucy-Kissan joulu: ISBN 978-9523189942, 2015

Lucy The Cat Bilingual Japanese – English, ISBN 978-1502399366, 2014
ねこのルーシー　バイリンガル　日本語－英語：
http://www.amazon.com/dp/B00O8II0LQ
Lucy The Cat and Little Brother Bilingual Japanese – English, ISBN 978-1503085022, 2014
ねこのルーシー　と　ちいさな　おとうと　バイリンガル　日本語－英語：
http://www.amazon.com/dp/B00SM1218S
Lucy The Cat Play With Me Bilingual Japanese – English, ISBN-13: 978-1511672931, 2015
ねこのルーシー　わたしと　あそんで　バイリンガル　日本語－英語：
http://www.amazon.com/dp/B00WWT82DO
Lucy The Cat And Little Kittens Bilingual Japanese – English , ISBN-13: 978-1517348137, 2015
ねこのルーシーと　ちいさな　こねこたち　バイリンガル：日本語 － 英語
http://www.amazon.com/dp/1517348137
Lucy The Cat Christmas Bilingual Japanese – English ISBN 978-1517754747, December 2015

Learn more about Lucy The Cat, other books and new releases:
http://www.pietarinen.org
https://www.facebook.com/lucythecat
https://www.facebook.com/GodsChildrenBook
https://www.facebook.com/KissaKiiskinen

Who is here under the hat?
Maybe you know me,
I'm Lucy The Cat.

And now I am back to tell you about my life.
Do you like holidays and what is your favorite one? I love especially Christmas. It's nice to see so many happy faces, colorful lights and all kind of decorations. And the presents!

People start Christmas preparations already weeks before. I don't know why, but it is fun to go to shops and find beautiful Christmas trees already in November. I would like to climb up to the top but my human dad does not allow me to do that.

And all those decorations and lights all over the city. I wish we had Christmas every day.

I have seen in TV that Christmas is very different in different parts of the world. Some places are sunny and hot and it is summer.

In other places Christmas is in the middle of the winter time and it is very cold and there is also a lot of snow. I am a cat and I prefer summer and sunshine.

I'm dreaming of a white Christmas. It looks so beautiful - at least if you don't need to go out. The nature is picturesque like a Christmas card.

Do you remember who is the most important animal in Christmas time. Of course Rudolph The Red-Nosed Reindeer. He has a very shiny nose. Without Rudolph Santa Claus would not be able to bring your presents. Once I saw some reindeers but Rudolph was not there.

Last Christmas I met Santa and he was so kind to me. I am sure you love Santa, too. I really want to meet him this Christmas again.

My human mom and dad are always busy when preparing for Christmas. There are so many things to do. You have to clean-up the house and prepare many kind of Christmas delicacies.

Mom also bakes many things. My favorite is the Gingerbread House. It is too small to enter. Maybe Moomin can go inside? Would you like to taste my Gingerbread House?

I am ready for the party but where are all the others? Where is the food?
Fish and beef, please!
And bring me some old cheddar cheese!

Time to decorate the house. I love to set-up Christmas tree and even more I like to play with candy canes, colorful balls, garlands, lametta, wreaths, snow flakes and all other decorations.

I always help mom and dad with the Christmas tree. It is fun to climb up and play a little. You may think it is dangerous but it is not. Oh, there is something wrong!

That candle was almost dropping down, but I fixed it. I am so skillful. Now I need to be careful not to fall down. The plastic branches are a bit slippery and you need to be careful with garlands and candy canes.

Dad went somewhere. Now it is time to play a little. When I hit the red ball with my paw it starts to swing. This is the real joy of Christmas. Would you like to play with me?

It is easy to play hide-and-seek in the tree. Mom did not find me and she called me:" Lucy, where are you?" Can you find me?

But finally the Christmas tree is complete for the Holiday season. And after all that playing and climbing in the tree it looks nice. Maybe some candles or candy canes are a bit …. But it is alright.

Maybe I should take a nap. After all it was hard work. But I love to help my human mom and dad. I am sure they are very happy to have so helpful cat.

Mom put the Christmas stockings on fireplace mantel piece. They are waiting to be filled. Maybe Santa comes during the night. What is your favorite present? I always love toys.

Santa came and put something into my stocking. I need to check out what it is. It is really exciting. What is it?

Wow! Thanks Santa!

One big mouse and three small ones. Or maybe the big one is a mole. Now I can play throughout the Christmas.

I love flowers. Poinsettias, amaryllis and other Christmas flowers are so beautiful. Poinsettias are poisonous and you can not eat them. One of my favorite chores is to water the flowers together with my mom. I always check if she has done it well.

I love to sing Christmas carols and songs with mom. I love music a lot and sometimes I even play piano. O Come All Ye Faithful Joyful and Triumphant, O Come Ye, O Come Ye to Bethlehem.

I think it's already quite late and I feel tired. Maybe it is time to go bed. My human mom and dad are still watching TV but there are no shows for cats.

I have to groom myself a little. I always want to be super clean. Do you take a shower every night before going to bed?

The Christmas tree looks still so colorful. Maybe I take it with me into my dreams. Oh Christmas tree, Oh Christmas tree! Thy leaves are so unchanging

Good night!
Have a joyful Christmas!

In my dreams I can see and hear the angels sing.
Silent night, Holy night
All is calm, all is bright ….

It is Christmas. Peace on earth for all! I wish you feel how love surrounds you and me and your mom and dad – everyone

64659148R00022